Published by Hachette Partworks Ltd
ISBN: 978-1-906965-29-7
Date of Printing: February 2011
Printed in Singapore by Tien Wah Press

The Fox and the Hound

Disney

Hachette

One spring morning, a mother fox dashed through a meadow carrying her baby. A hunter and his dogs were chasing them and the mother fox needed to find a safe place to hide her cub.

The mother fox soon came to a patch of tall grass. She covered up her baby and ran away, hoping that the dogs would follow her. The dogs came sniffing through the grass, but they did not see the frightened baby fox.

When the hunter and his
dogs had gone, the baby fox
poked his tiny nose out of the
grass and sniffed around. The
little fox waited and waited,
but there was no sign of
his mother.

Luckily, a kindly owl
named Big Mama had seen
everything. She flew down
to comfort the little fox.
"Now, don't you
worry," said the gentle
owl. "Big Mama will
find someone else to
take care of you."

Big Mama quickly
found her two friends,
Dinky the sparrow and
Boomer the woodpecker.

"Please help me," said
Big Mama. "We must
find a new home for this
little fox."

Dinky and Boomer
had been trying to catch
a caterpillar for their
dinner, but they stopped
to help Big Mama.

"What can we do to
help the little fellow?"
they asked, while the
caterpillar quietly
crawled away.

"We'll lead that nice Widow Tweed right to him,"
Big Mama explained. "She'll know what to do then."
And so Big Mama and Boomer grabbed a piece of
Widow Tweed's washing from her clothesline. When
the widow ran after the birds, they dropped the
clothing right on top of the baby fox.

"Goodness!" cried Widow Tweed when she spotted the baby fox. "What are you doing here?"

The warm-hearted widow loved the little fox at once.
"You're just like a toddler," said Widow Tweed. "I
think I will call you Tod for short." Tod liked the widow
and his new name very much.

Not far from the
widow's house lived a
hunter named Amos.
He had just come
home with a puppy.

"His name is Copper,"
Amos told his old dog Chief.
"He'll be a big help to us
when he grows up."
But Chief did not
want any help and
he pretended not
to care about
Copper.

When Copper curled up beside Chief and fell asleep, Chief decided that the puppy wasn't so bad after all.

As Copper grew up, he became very curious about the world around him. One day, as he went sniffing through the forest...

... he found himself nose-to-nose with a fox!

"My name is Copper," said the puppy.
"My name is Tod," said the little fox.

And before the day
was over, the fox and
the hound were the best
of friends.

That evening, Amos the
hunter was very angry
when Copper came home.
He decided to tie up
Copper, so that the puppy
could not get away from his
kennel again.

Tod hid in the bushes
and watched. He was very
sad to see his new friend
in trouble.

Tod decided to visit
his friend to cheer him
up. But as soon as Chief
smelled the fox, he began
to chase him.

When Amos saw Chief chasing Tod,
the hunter was sure that Tod was
after his chickens. So Amos chased Tod
all the way to Widow Tweed's house.

"You keep that fox away from my chickens!"
Amos shouted angrily at Widow Tweed.

"You leave Tod alone!" Widow Tweed
declared. "He would never hurt your chickens.
Now go away!"

Tod was very
frightened, and so
was the widow.
She knew that Tod
would get hurt if he
went near Amos's
property again.

"Tod, you'd better
stay in the house," she
said sadly.

A few days later, Tod watched from Widow
Tweed's window as Amos packed for a hunting trip.
Tod was even sadder when he saw his friend Copper
disappear from view as Amos drove away.

As the weeks passed, Copper learned how to be a hunting dog, just like Chief.

Soon Copper was no longer a puppy, but
a full-grown dog with a nose that could
track anything!

Back home, Tod grew tired of waiting for Copper to come back. He decided to pay a visit to Amos's house to see if they had returned.

On the way he ran into his old friend Big Mama.

"Be careful," she warned. "Copper is grown up, just like you. His job is to chase foxes now. He can't be your friend any more."

Tod didn't believe that Copper could have changed that much.

At last, Copper came home. He sat in the
front seat with Amos, howling as only a dog
can howl. Chief just covered his ears.

That night, Tod heard Copper's howling and
ran over to greet his pal.

Copper was surprised to see Tod, but sadly
told him to go away.

"We can't be the best of friends any more,"
Copper tried to explain. "I have a job to do, and
that job is to hunt foxes!"

Tod tried to argue, but Chief suddenly began
to bark.

Tod tried to get away from Chief. He zigzagged as fast as he could, but another dog was right behind him. It was Copper! The dogs had got loose!

"I won't let him find you," Copper barked. "Run to the bridge. I'll lead him the other way."

But Chief was a smart old hunting dog. He was waiting for Tod on the bridge. Moments later, a rumble surprised them both. Chief and Tod looked up to see a train coming towards them at full speed!

Tod squeezed into a tiny space as the train roared past. But Chief was not so lucky. He was forced right off the bridge by the speeding train.

When Copper found Chief, he blamed Tod.
"This is what happens when you're friends with a fox," Copper thought angrily. "I won't let him get away again."

Tod was very frightened. As soon as he
returned home, he curled up in Widow
Tweed's arms. Suddenly, Amos pounded on
the door.

"Your fox almost got my dog killed tonight!"
Amos shouted at the widow. "He's a nasty,
wild animal!"

Widow Tweed shouted back at Amos,
"*You're* the nasty one! Leave us alone!"

Widow Tweed knew that Amos was right about Tod being a wild animal. He didn't belong on a farm any longer. He needed to be free.

She brought Tod to a safe place in the woods and hugged him.

"This will be your home now, Tod," she said sadly. "It will be better for you here." Tod watched her go, feeling very lonely and sad.

But he wasn't alone for long. His old friend Big Mama was watching out for him, and she led him to a lovely lady fox named Vixey.

Soon Tod had a new best friend!

One day, the two young foxes heard gunshots.
It was Amos and Copper out hunting.
"Run, Vixey!" Tod shouted as they dashed away.

The loud growl of a bear interrupted the chase. Suddenly, the angry bear rushed towards all of them. Shocked, Amos stepped back – right into a steel trap!

Copper bravely tried to protect his master, but the tough old bear threw the faithful dog to the ground.

Tod stopped running when he heard Copper's barking. "Copper tried to help me once," he remembered. He raced back to try to save his old friend from the angry bear.

The bear forgot about Copper as he
chased Tod to the river. Tod tried to
escape across an old log, but when the
bear followed him, the log broke.
Tod and the bear plunged into
the cold water below!

Tod pulled
himself to the
bank, only to find
Amos aiming his
gun right at him!

Copper couldn't let Amos hurt Tod. Quickly, he
stood in Amos's way, protecting his friend.

Amos lowered his gun. "You're right," he said.
"The fox saved us from the bear." Copper then went
and stood by Amos as they watched Tod escape.

When Widow Tweed saw Amos limping home, she hurried out to see what had happened. As she bandaged his hurt foot, Amos told her about Tod, Copper and the bear.

"I was wrong," said Amos. "Your fox is nice, after all."

Widow Tweed just smiled. She knew that Tod would be safe from Amos from now on.

A few days later, Tod
and Vixey sat on a cliff
overlooking the valley.
They looked down at their
friends and wished them
happiness.

"Now I know what the
two most beautiful things
in the world are," Tod
told Vixey. "Love and
friendship."

Tod and Vixey agreed
that they were lucky to
have both.